This was one weird cat ...

Her eyes grew wider, and you know how cat eyes are sometimes black in the center? That's the way they were—two glowing circles of greenish-yellow light, with darkness at the centers.

She floated up to a standing position, and then the middle of her back kept going up, making the kind of hump that cats make when they're mad or crazy. And she opened her mouth, showed her spiky little teeth, and cut loose with an eerie yowl.

The Case of
the Vampire Cat

John R. Erickson

Illustrations by Gerald L. Holmes

Puffin Books

PUFFIN BOOKS
Published by the Penguin Group
Penguin Putnam Books for Young Readers,
345 Hudson Street, New York, New York 10014, U.S.A.
Penguin Books Ltd,
27 Wrights Lane, London W8 5TZ, England
Penguin Books Australia Ltd,
Ringwood, Victoria, Australia
Penguin Books Canada Ltd,
10 Alcorn Avenue, Toronto, Ontario, Canada M4V 3B2
Penguin Books (N.Z.) Ltd,
182-190 Wairau Road, Auckland 10, New Zealand

Penguin Books Ltd, Registered Offices:
Harmondsworth, Middlesex, England

First published in the United States of America
by Maverick Books, Gulf Publishing Company, 1993
Published by Puffin Books, a member of
Penguin Putnam Books for Young Readers, 1999

10

LIBRARY OF CONGRESS CATALOGING-IN-PUBLICATION DATA
Erickson, John R., date
The case of the vampire cat / John R. Erickson ;
illustrations by Gerald L. Holmes.
p. cm.
Previously published: Houston, Tex. : Maverick Books, c1993.
(Hank the Cowdog ; 21)
Summary: Hank the Cowdog, Head of Ranch Security, bravely faces the
dangers of Picket Canyon to unravel the mystery surrounding an unusual cat.
ISBN 0-14-130397-2 (pbk.)
[1. Dogs Fiction. 2. Cats Fiction. 3. Ranch life—West (U.S.) Fiction.
4. West (U.S.) Fiction. 5. Mystery and detective stories. 6. Humorous stories.]
I. Holmes, Gerald L., ill. II. Title. III. Series: Erickson, John R., date
Hank the Cowdog ; #21
[PZ7.E72556Cav 1999] [Fic]—dc21 99-19582 CIP

Printed in the United States of America

To Clayton Umbach, Director of Gulf Publishing Company's Book Division, who has been Hank's friend since the early days

CONTENTS

CHAPTER ONE

Frozen Water, No Coffee

It's me again, Harry the Hog Dog. Not really. I just thought I'd give you a little shock there and test to make sure you were wide awake and ready for the exciting story of how I escaped from the depths of Picket Canyon.

Because you'd better be ready for this one. See, I got stranded and abandoned on the Hodges' Place and had to find my way back home, in a snowstorm mind you, had to find my way back home in this terrible snowstorm.

And in case you haven't been lost and abandoned in Picket Canyon lately, let me tell you that it's a very scary place, especially when the sun goes down, and the coyotes are as thick as hair on a dog. So you'd better get yourself pre-

1

pared for a double-scary story, and maybe you shouldn't read it at all unless you're Certified Tough.

Oh, and did I mention the cat? Maybe not. There was this cat named Mary D and she'd been marooned on the Hodges' Place for years, staying down there all by herself, you see, and boy, was she weird.

She was so weird, she'd turned into a VAMPIRE. No kidding.

I told you this was going to be a scary story.

But I seem to be getting the pony before the horse. Better go back and start at the beginning.

Where was I?

Oh yes. It's me again, Hank the Cowdog. It was sometime in the middle of February, and as you might know, that is a month when we often get snow in the Texas Panhandle, and when I awoke that morning and looked out the window at Slim's shack, that's what I saw.

Big snowflakes falling from the sky.

Drover and I had spent the night down at Slim's place because . . . well, it should be obvious. Slim was a soft-hearted cowboy who took pity on poor ranch dogs who had to sleep out in the weather, and he'd invited us to bunk at his camp.

He allowed us to sleep beside the wood-burning

stove, don't you see, and even though I'm opposed in principle to the idea of . . .

It makes a dog soft, all that luxury, and soft is okay for your town dogs and your poodles and your little yip-yip breeds, but cowdogs need to be tough. And sleeping inside the house beside a nice warm stove is . . .

Well, it's pretty nice, to tell you the truth, and once in a while a guy has to compromise his principles for . . . I did it mainly for Drover, see. He's something of a yip-yip, has a stub tail and short hair, and in cold weather he whines and moans and shivers all night, and who can sleep with all that noise?

And so, in a gesture of deepest concern for Drover's health and so forth, I agreed to sleep down at Slim's place, beside the wood-burning stove. But I let Mister Moan-and-Groan know that we couldn't make a habit of it.

Staying down at Slim's place is kind of fun, actually, when a guy gets over the notion that he's being corrupted by luxury. There's always a mouse or two to chase before bedtime, and sometimes, if it's a particularly cold night, old Slim lets us dogs sleep in the bed with him.

The only problem there is that Slim snores in his sleep, and he's bad about stealing covers and throwing elbows. Oh yes, and I once caught fleas in his bed.

Anyways, we got up that morning around daylight, which came a little later than usual because the sky was so dark and cloudy. I heard Slim coming out of his bedroom and down the hall.

He was his usual jolly self in the morning: eyes half-open, hair down in his face, little balls of lint in his beard, bouncing off the walls as he staggered down the dark hall in search of the coffeepot.

He made it to the kitchen and found the stove. He found the box of matches. He lit a match, lit a burner on the stove, found the coffee, turned on the water faucet, and . . . nothing came out. I raised my ears and rolled my eyes around and waited.

There was a long throbbing silence, followed by a deep sigh of deepest despair. Then, "Thanks, Lord. I guess I needed the water to be froze up this morning. I'm sure you wouldn't do that to a poor old cowboy without a good reason.

"Dadgum water! I knew I should have wrapped them pipes. I knew it would turn off cold one of these days and I'd get caught, and sure 'nuff, I did."

He wandered out into the room where we were. He sure looked lost and pitiful. I mean, here was a guy who was having to face the cold cruel world

4

without a cup of coffee, and even though I don't drink coffee myself, I know it's important to these cowboys.

He yawned, raked the hair out of his eyes, and shuffled over to the stove. That's when he greeted me with his first words of the day: "Move, pooch, or I'll chunk up the stove with your carcass."

Not "Good morning, Hank," or "Hi, doggie," or "Thanks for protecting the house last night, Hank." Oh no. Just "Move, pooch, or I'll chunk up the stove with your carcass."

And I, being an intelligent dog and not wanting to be chunked or stoved, moved my carcass—and just barely in time to avoid being clunked on the head by the stove door when he opened it.

He opened it and peeked inside. "Huh. Still got a few coals of bodark left. Good." He reached into his wood box, brought out some bark, twigs, and kindling, and tossed them into the stove. He blew on the coals. Then he . . .

That was strange. He jerked his head back, jumped to his feet, and started . . . this was very strange . . . started slapping himself on the face! Now, why would he . . .

Okay, I've got it now. See, Slim used big chunks of bodark in his stove at night. Bodark, being the very hardest wood on the ranch, made the best all-nighter logs for the stove, because the hardest wood burns the longest.

The only problem with bodark is that it tends to pop and make sparks, and that's not exactly what Slim was thinking about when he got down on his hands and knees and blew on the embers. They popped and threw a spark into his beard, and that's why he was slapping himself on the face.

Putting out the spark, don't you see.

Well, he got the kindling going and added a few small sticks of cottonwood and a few medium-sized chunks of hackberry. He closed up the stove, opened the draft and the damper, and wandered over to the window. That's when he saw the snow.

"Thanks, Lord. I sure needed some snow, since my plumbing is froze up and I have to step out on the porch." He scratched his beard for a moment. "Guess I could put on my slippers, but I'd have to walk all the way back to the bedroom. Too much trouble."

He yawned, went to the door, and stepped out on the porch. He came back a whole lot faster than he went out, and he ran to the stove on crumpled toes and stood there, shivering and warming his hands. Then his eyes fell on me.

"You need to go out too, Muttfuzz. I don't want to be steppin' on any surprises this morning."

Well, uh, I really didn't care much for the idea of going out into the frozen cold and snow and so forth, and if it was okay . . .

"Out! Come on. You too, Stub Tail."

And so it was that we were tossed out of house and hearth. It was bad enough, just going out into the cold and snow, but on top of that, I had to listen to Drover's moaning and groaning. He took two steps off the porch and locked down in his tracks, and there he stood, crying and whining.

Not me. I made a quick tour of the area, checked out the grounds, sniffed a few trees, and, yes, it was pretty cold and miserable out there, so I hurried back to the front of the house and stationed myself right in front of the picture window, where Slim couldn't miss seeing me.

There, I went into a little routine called "We're Freezing Out Here," which consists of Shivers, Sad Eyes, Slow Wags, and Heavy Begs. It's a cracker-jack routine and it should have worked.

I mean, there I was, standing out in the frozen wastes of Antarctica, and there he was, pulling on his red long-john underwear in front of a nice warm stove. I could see him in there, and *he saw me out there*. I know he did because he waved at me, and I saw his lips move and form the words "Hi, puppy." And then he grinned.

He thinks he's so funny. Hi, puppy! Who did he think he was? How would he have felt if . . . oh well.

The Heavy Begs routine didn't work. We stayed out in the snow and the frozen tundra, shivering and so forth, until he had put on all his layers of clothes and came out of the house.

He was wearing galoshes, a sheeplined coat, and his wool cap with the ear flappers. He fired up the pickup and we were ready to drive up to headquarters and begin the day.

And what a day it turned out to be.

CHAPTER TWO

Loper Melts
a Water Pipe

W̲ell, at least he was kind and decent enough to let us ride in the cab with him, although it wouldn't have surprised me if he'd made us ride in the back.

He has this strange theory, you see, that snow makes dogs wet and wet dogs stink. I've tested that theory myself and I can report that it just doesn't hold water, so to speak. If you ask me, wet cowboys stink, but nobody ever asks my opinion.

He let us ride in the front, and we made our way through the snow and ice to headquarters. Along the way, we passed several bunches of cows. Their backs were covered with snow, and they were humped up and facing away from the north wind. And every time they breathed, which

9

was fairly often, their breath made fog in the air.

Yes, it was a cold, miserable day, and according to the weather report Slim picked up on the radio, the day promised to get even colder and miserabler.

When he heard the report, he pressed his lips together and shook his head. "And I have to face all that without a cup of coffee."

We pulled around in front of the machine shed and came to a stop beside the water well. Loper was there, doing something with the cutting torch, and whatever he was doing didn't appear to be bringing him much happiness. He wore a frown.

Slim watched him for a moment. "Plumbing froze up?"

Loper looked up from his work. "Yeah. You got any cute remarks about it?"

"No, only that if you'd take the time to wrap them pipes when it's warm, they wouldn't freeze up when it's cold."

"No kidding? Thanks." He went back to heating the pipe with the torch.

"This happens every year, Loper. A good ranch manager would catch on after a while. You'll notice that my pipes don't freeze. That's because I take care of my business."

What? I stared at Slim and thumped my tail on the seat. Unless I had heard him wrong, he had just told a big whopper of a lie. His water pipes HAD frozen up, that very morning.

Slim's gaze shifted to me. "Hush. What he don't know won't help him." Back to Loper. "You know, Loper, I was thawing out pipes with a torch one time and burned a hole in the pipe. Boy, that sure makes a mess."

Loper turned off the torch and came over to the window. "Do you want to do it?"

"Not really."

"Good. I'll do it and you can either watch or go do something constructive, but don't sit there in a warm pickup and give me advice."

"Well, you don't need to get snarly about it. I was just trying to help."

"Thanks. When I need your advice on plumbing, I'll give you a call. We've got phones, you know."

"I know how you operate, Loper: slam-bang and always in a rush. That's the wrong way to thaw out pipes."

Loper went back to the torch, shaking his head and talking to himself. "No wonder you're still a bachelor. No woman could stand you in the morning."

"Well, you ain't such a sugar cake yourself, if you want to know the truth, and I've often wondered how Sally May has put up with you all these years."

Loper started the torch again and tuned in the flame. "She's a very lucky woman and she knows it."

"That's too much fire, Loper."

"Just hush, Slim. Control yourself for two minutes and I'll have this thing thawed out, and then we'll find some little job for you to . . ."

By George, he struck water.

Slim shook his head. "I tried to tell you."

Loper shut off the torch and threw it down in the

snow and came storming over to the window. "Get
me a hacksaw with a sharp blade, and don't say one
more word. It was a sorry pipe to start with."

Slim got out. "Sure it was. What are you going
to fix it with, bubble gum?"

Loper was scrambling to shut off the main water
valve. "Get me one of those compression joints off
the workbench. And if it's not too much trouble,
why don't you hurry."

It took 'em an hour to fix the pipe. They had to
cut out the bad section with a hacksaw. The blade
was not sharp. I could have predicted that. This
ranch has never had a sharp hacksaw blade. I
think they buy dull blades at a special store.

Once they got the pipe cut out, the rest was
fairly easy. They slipped the compression joint
over both ends and tightened them down. They
pressured up the lines, stopped all the leaks, and
hollered down for Sally May to turn on a faucet.

She did. It worked. The job was done, and Slim
and Loper had managed to do it without any
bloodshed. Sally May even brought out cups of coffee for the "heroes," as she called them.

I waited to see if Slim would admit that this was
his first cup of the morning, and then explain why,
but he didn't.

Well, the boys put up their tools and stood at

the door of the machine shed, sipping their coffee and watching the snow come down.

"Well, what do you reckon?" asked Loper.

"Radio says more this afternoon and tonight. It's liable to take us all day to feed and bust ice."

"I think what we'd better do is split up. I'll take the flatbed and get Sally May to drive for me, and we'll feed hay up north. You take the old pickup down to the Hodges' Place and feed there. You probably better use the army truck, bad as those roads are liable to be."

Slim nodded. "What if it won't start?"

"Well . . . why don't you take Alfred? He can pull you. He's done that before, and then he can drive while you string out the feed."

"Okay with me, but his momma might not go for the idea of me taking him off in a snowstorm, and I've got a few questions about that myself. I'd hate to get stranded with him along."

Loper chuckled. "Why, he's a nice boy, Slim. You two would have a ball together."

"I know he's a nice boy. That ain't the problem. I just hate being responsible for somebody else's child in a storm."

Loper gazed up at the clouds. "Well, I think we're going to need all the help we can get today. I'll clear it with his momma. Oh, and you can take the dogs."

"Thanks a bunch. Two wet dogs and one urchin child ought to fix me right up."

Loper went back to the house to organize the troops. Slim finished his coffee and then pulled the flatbed pickup around to the hay lot and started loading it up for Loper. The snow was coming down harder than ever.

While I looked for mice under the bales, Drover stood out in the snow, shivering and moaning.

"Oh Hank, I'm so cold! I wish I could go back to bed."

"Drover, if wishes were horses, beggars would ride."

"I don't know what that means, and I'm freezing!"

"It means that if you could turn your fondest wish into a horse, you could . . . I don't know, give some beggar a ride into town, I guess."

"Where would you go to find a beggar in this weather?"

"Well, you'd just . . . how should I know? Quit asking silly questions and catch some mice."

"I don't even know what a beggar is, and I'm too cold to care."

"A beggar, son, is one who begs."

"One *what*?"

"One beggar. A beggar is one beggar who begs. That's simple enough."

"Why are they going to town?"

"Because they . . . I don't know. They need a horse, I guess."

"I thought horses lived in the country."

"They do live in the country but . . . never mind, Drover, just never mind. I'm sorry I brought it up."

"Oh, that's okay, but I'm still freezing."

After that, I stayed as far away from Drover as I could. Just being close to him made me feel goofy.

Little Alfred arrived on the scene just then. He was all dressed up in a red snowsuit, red mittens, snow boots, and a wool stocking cap.

Slim got the hay loaded, just about the time Loper and Sally May and Baby Molly arrived. Alfred had been cleared by Headquarters to go with us to the Hodges' Place, but Sally May still had quite a bit of advice to give Slim about being careful.

Then we all said good-bye and went our separate ways. Loper and his bunch went north to feed hay, and Slim and our bunch loaded up in the old blue pickup and headed south.

When we passed Miss Viola's house down the creek, Slim honked his horn and said, "That's where my petunia lives." We didn't see his petunia, but her two dogs, Black and Jack, came ripping out of the driveway and barked at us.

Well, you know me. I don't take such things lightly. I sprang to the window and barked back at them, and if the window glass hadn't been rolled up, I probably would have thrashed them both, right there in the middle of the county road.

Nothing makes me madder than . . .

Hmmm. Slim stopped the pickup and opened his door, and then he said to me . . . I think he was addressing me . . . he said, "You really want a piece of those dogs?"

I, uh . . . no, that was okay. There was no actual law against . . . heck, as long as they just barked and didn't . . . no, we'd let it slide this time.

In other words, no thanks.

"Then hush." He slammed his door and started off again.

Fine. I could handle that. Hushing had never been a problem for me.

17

CHAPTER THREE

We Meet the Weirdest Cat You Ever Saw

Have I mentioned that Loper had taken a lease on the Hodges' ranch? Maybe not, but he had, and we were wintering a bunch of cows on it. It was a dandy place to winter cows, because all the canyons and rough country gave them protection from storms.

But it wasn't such a dandy place to reach in a two-wheel-drive pickup, in a snowstorm. Once you left the blacktop highway up on the flats, you faced nine miles of long, lonesome road, without a single house to mark the way or give you the feeling that you could get help if you needed it.

And there were spots in that long, lonesome

18

road where a guy could get himself stuck. Slim came pretty close on several occasions. The road was bad and getting worse.

The road came to an end at the little camp house. When we got there, Slim shut off the pickup and took a deep breath.

"Whoo boy! I wasn't sure we were going to get here. We shouldn't have tried to make it down here without a four-wheel-drive. It's a good thing we've got the Cammo-Stealth army truck down here. Let's see if she'll start."

We all piled out of the blue pickup and moved over to the Cammo-Stealth army truck. What was the Cammo-Stealth army truck? A 1953 Dodge 4 x 4 with big mudgrip tires all the way around, a six-cylinder engine, and a four-speed transmission. It had a canvas top and was painted camouflage colors.

That's where the "Cammo" part of the name came from. The "Stealth" part came from . . . let's see if I can remember what Slim told Little Alfred . . . the old truck was so well camouflaged that it was "invisible to enemy radar."

That's what he said, and if you want to know who the "enemy" was and why they were using radar on the ranch, you'll have to ask Slim.

Actually, I think it was some kind of joke.

Anyways, we hiked over to the Cammo-Stealth, which was parked on the west side of the camp house. Slim climbed in under the wheel and called Little Alfred over to watch.

"Pay attention, Button. I may get hurt down here one of these days and need you to drive me to town. I want you to know how to start this old thing."

The boy climbed up on the running board. "Okay, Swim."

"First thing you do when you drive any vehicle is check the gas gauge, only the gas gauge don't work on this truck, so you run a shovel handle into the tank. Here, I'd better show you."

He got out and ran a shovel handle into the tank. He pulled it out and showed the boy the wet mark. "That means you've got about ten gallons of gas."

He got back inside and went through the whole starting routine: put the gearshift into neutral; pull out the ignition switch; pull out the choke as far as it will go, but don't press on the gas pedal, "'cause this thing will flood if you even say 'gas pedal.'"

"What does 'fwuud' mean?"

"It means the motor won't start because . . . I don't know why. Just do what I tell you and never mind the how-come."

It was then that the cat appeared. Description: female calico, medium height and weight, longhair, pink nose, long white cat whiskers, and a pair of eyes that were something between greenish and yellowish.

They called her Mary D Cat.

She crawled out from under the house and came running toward us—yowling. Now, most of your ranch cats will yowl once in a while but not all the time. This one, once she started a yowl, she hung on to it and didn't quit.

It wasn't a short and simple "meow." It was more like "Meeeee-yowwwwwwwwww."

Well, Drover and I were standing there beside the Cammo-Stealth, listening to Slim's lecture. The cat came bounding over to us, and right away I noticed that she didn't have much respect for a dog.

I mean, most of your ranch cats will approach a dog with some caution. They should. Not only is that the proper and mannerly thing to do, but it is the smart thing to do.

See, some dogs don't need much of an excuse to thrash a cat. You might even say that we . . . uh, they . . . you might even say that they consider pounding cats part of their job. Or even a form of sport—a good, clean, wholesome sport that all the family can enjoy.

And for that reason, your smart cats . . . or to put it another way, your cats who are less dumb than the dumber ones will NOT come bounding up to a dog they've never met before, because that is a really stupid thing to do and it can get a cat into deep trouble.

But this one? Here she came, bounding straight toward us and yowling.

"A crust of bread? Baloney, cheese?
Spare a morsel, if you please.
Marooned, I am, oh hateful place!
At last I've found a friendly face!"

Well, this was very strange. She came right up to me and began rubbing on my leg and yowling in my face. I guess you know how much I love being rubbed on by cats. I don't. But there she was, all over me, just as though we were old friends, and we weren't. Not yet and maybe never.

"A crust of bread? Baloney, cheese? Spare a morsel, if you please."

I pushed her away. "Uh, Kitty, I think there's been some . . . I don't have any cheese. No cheese, no baloney, no bread, and *would you please stop rubbing on me!*"

She went right on. "Marooned I am, oh hateful place! At last I've found a friendly face!"

I backed up several steps to get away from . . .
fellers, this was a weird cat! I'd been rubbed on
by cats before, but nothing like this. I backed up
to get away from her, but there she was again—
rubbing, purring, and yowling about cheese.

"Kitty, I'm sorry you've been marooned and I
guess you think you've found a friendly face after
all these years, but . . . get back, will you? I think
you've made a slight error. That is, I think you've
mistaken my face for . . . WILL YOU STOP RUB-
BING ON ME!"

"Cheese, just one little piece of cheese. I dream
of cheese, you know. And baloney. And Vienna
sausage. And sir, you have such a friendly face, I
just know you won't turn me away."

I was baffled. I mean, what can you do with a
cat that is half-starved, half-crazy, and trying to
love you to death? You can't just beat her up and
go on about your business.

I solved the problem by surrendering my spot.
I ran around to the other side of the army truck
and waited to see what Drover would do. When I
left, Kitty didn't miss a beat. She moved right in
on Drover and started the same routine about
cheese and a friendly face.

Drover wasted no time with niceties or small

talk. He didn't know what was wrong with this cat but he knew something was screwy, and he wasn't going to take any chances. You'd have thought he was facing a python or a boa constrictor or a ghost.

Zoom! He vanished. Kitty had just lost another friendly face. Not one to be discouraged, she went straight to the Cammo-Stealth and jumped up on Slim's lap. He was deep into his lesson on starting the truck.

"Okay, you pull out the choker, let 'er sit for a minute, then . . ." He pitched the cat away. "Then you mash down on the starter . . ." The cat was back in his lap. ". . . with your foot, like this here."

He pitched the cat and pushed on the starter. It turned over with a growl. The cat jumped back on his lap. He pitched her again. The motor continued to turn. Then it fired once. The cat was back in his lap.

Slim stopped what he was doing and looked down at her. She rubbed her ear across his chin and then flicked her tail over his nose.

"Kitty, I know you love me and I don't blame you 'cause I'm so wonderful, but we're fixing to have a problem. I can't start this truck with your tail in my face. Now scram."

He pitched her out, and two seconds later, she was right back. "Button, will you get this love-crazed cat out of here? 'Cause if you don't, I'll be forced to break her heart and possibly her neck."

Little Alfred took charge of the cat problem, and right away I could see that he had just the right approach. Holding her in a loving headlock, he began dragging her around through the snow. And it worked. The cat just went limp, didn't fight or scratch or struggle or make any kind of protest.

Well, with the cat under control, Slim turned back to the problem of starting the truck, which sounded as though it didn't want to start. He hit the starter again and the motor turned over and over, until at last it kicked off.

I had the misfortune of standing near the exhaust pipe when the motor kicked off, and it may be years before I get all of that blue smoke out of my lungs. Boy, that was quite a . . . COUGH, HARK, ARG . . . quite a cloud of smoke, and I decided to move my business around to the front.

Slim revved up the motor and adjusted the choke and told Alfred to get in—without the cat. Then they pulled around to the cake house and started loading sacks of feed.

I followed and heaved a sigh of relief. At last we were rid of the . . .

You'll never guess who went streaking past me and headed straight for the cake house. I'll give you a hint. She was calico-colored and weird.

Yes, it was the cat.

Perhaps you know where I stand on the issue of letting cats pass me on the way to the cake house. I don't allow it. It sets a bad example, don't you see, and can lead to trouble later on. Cats should always be last.

So I reached for the afterburners and hit full-throttle and went streaking through the snow. And she beat me to the cake house.

Hmmm. That was a pretty fast cat.

CHAPTER FOUR

The Kitty Is Lured into My Trap

But of course we mustn't forget that there were other circumstances involved.

Did I think to mention that I pulled a muscle in my right hind leg? Oh yes, bad muscle pull. I hadn't warmed up, see, and the cat had probably spent all morning warming up and preparing for that sprint to the cake house, so one interpretation of the facts is that she, well, cheated.

Or if she hadn't actually cheated, she had certainly taken unfair advantage of the situation. Hey, I had a steady job, many things to do besides warm up for a silly little race to the cake house, which, in the larger scheme of things, meant almost nothing anyway.

I mean, who cared, really? Life is filled with

challenges, and racing a rinky-dink cat ranks very far down the list.

And did I mention about the cockleburs? Yes. Not only was I slowed by a tragic injury to the Greater Boogaloo muscle in my right posterior thigh, which would have put most dogs out of the race right there, but once the race began, I found myself running over gobs and gobs of dangerous cockleburs.

You ever try to run a hard race on cockleburs? It's virtually impossible. You talk about pain! No ordinary dog could have stayed in that race. I not only stayed in the race but finished a respectable second, and might very well have won if it had gone on another twenty feet.

And if the cat hadn't cheated and used underhanded tricks to . . . but the important point is that the race meant nothing to me, and finishing second to a stupid cat sure didn't damage my self-esteamer, and just to prove how insignificant the whole thing was to me, I went over to the cat and gave her my congratulations for a race well run.

"Kitty," I said between gulps of air, "as a small token of my admiration for your athletic ability, I am going to make sausage patties out of you."

A lot of cats will run when you, uh, offer them such a small token. This one whirled around, humped up, hissed, stared at me with those strange yellowish eyes, and said, "Listen, clown, you lay a paw on me and I'll take out your eyeballs and feed 'em to the crows!"

"Huh?"

"And don't think I can't do it."

I, uh, took several steps backward. "Settle down, sister. I think perhaps you . . ."

"I've been marooned on this ranch for two long years. I've survived coons, coyotes, bobcats, skunks, badgers, hawks, eagles, and rattlesnakes."

"Well, sure, and I admire that . . . in a certain limited sense."

"You may think you're tough, potlicker, but you won't know what that word means until you lay a paw on me."

I cleared my throat. "You know, I sense that we're barking up the wrong road here, and perhaps you misappropriated my meaning. All I meant to say was that, well, you run a pretty good race . . . for a cat."

She studied me with those unblinking cattish eyes. "What about the sausage business?"

"The sausage business? Oh that. Ha, ha. It

meant nothing, almost nothing at all, just a little attempt at humor. Ha, ha."

She heaved a sigh and relaxed the hump in her back. "It's been so long since I tasted sausage!"

"Right, exactly, and that was my whole point, you see. I was just saying, wouldn't it be nice to have a bite of sausage and . . ." I leaned forward and whispered, ". . . cheese."

The word had a dramatic effect on the stupid . . . on Miss Mary D Cat. All at once her pink little mouth curled up in a smile. She closed her eyes, began to purr, and started rubbing on my leg.

"Cheese! Oh, what I'd give for a piece of cheese! I dream of cheese, you know, and . . .

"A crust of bread? Baloney, cheese?
Spare a morsel, if you please.
Marooned, I am, oh hateful place!
At last I've found a friendly face!"

Hmm, very interesting. It appeared that I had stumbled onto a classic case of Skipsofrazzled Personality, and in case you're not familiar with these heavy-duty technical terms, let me explain.

Your typical Skipsofrazzled Personality skips from one mood to another, don't you see. They'll

30

be chirpy one minute and the next minute they'll be yowling and hissing, and in your extreme cases, they'll even make boastful threats such as "I'll tear out your eyeballs and feed 'em to the crows."

Another trait or characteristic of your Skipsofrazzled Personality is that the skipping mechanism can be activated by a certain code word. And you will notice that it took me only a matter of seconds to sniff out and discover Mary D Cat's code word.

Heh, heh.

Cheese.

Heh, heh.

Pretty clever, huh? And now I can reveal for the first time that the so-called "Race to the Cake House" was just a ploy I had used to gather important information about this weird little cat.

That's correct. I had planned it from the start, and losing the race was just part of the overall stragedy.

Are you shocked? Surprised? Heh, heh. Don't ever underestimate the cunning of a Head of Ranch Security, and don't forget that we spend a good part of our time operating underground. And don't forget that staying at least one step ahead of the kittens is just part of my job.

Okay, where were we? Oh yes, I had just outsmarted and outflanked Mary D Cat and had gathered crucial information I needed. And now she was purring and rubbing on my legs and driving me nuts, and once again I found myself thinking, "GET AWAY FROM ME!"

But rather than coming right out and saying that, which would have been tacky and un-friendly—and, well, might have caused her to skip back over to the "Tear Out Your Eyeballs" skinario—I elected to, well, flee.

Surrender my spot.

Run around to the back of the cake house. And guess who or whom I found hiding back there. Mister Shivers.

He greeted me with his usual simple grin. "Oh, hi Hank."

"What are you doing back here?"

"Oh . . . watching the snowflakes fall, I guess. And shivering."

"I see. Is there some reason why you can't shiver and watch the snowflakes around front with the rest of us?"

"Well . . . I guess I wanted to get away from that cat. I just don't know what to do or say when she starts rubbing on me."

"She's just trying to be friendly, Drover."

"Yeah, but she gives me the creeps. I never met a cat like her."

"Yes, well, you must understand, Drover, that she's been living out here by herself for years and she doesn't know how to respond to the sudden appearance of dogs who are . . . well, highly intelligent, dashing, daring, donder, blitsen, and handsome."

"Yeah, that's me, all right."

I glared at the runt. "Actually, I had myself in mind, but since you've brought up the subject of the cat . . ."

I placed a paw on his shoulder and led him a few steps away. There, I glanced around to be sure we weren't being watched and conducted the rest of the conversation in a whisper.

"Since you brought up the subject of the cat, I wonder if you might do a little job for me."

"What little job?"

"Actually, Drover, it's not so little, and in fact, it's a mission of great importance."

"Gosh, and you'd let me do it?"

"That's correct. I've had my eye on you for a long time, Drover, with this particular mission in mind, and I'm proud to tell you that I think you're ready for it."

He puffed himself up and beamed with pride. "Gosh, I'm so happy and proud, I don't know what to say."

"I understand, son, and saying nothing will be just fine."

"But if it's such an important mission, how come you'd trust me with it?"

"Because . . ." I began pacing, as I often do when I'm reaching into the gaseous clouds of vapor and trying to find the right words to express a deep thought. "Because, Drover, it's time. It's time for you to take on more responsibility. And it's time for me to allow you to take on more responsibility."

Suddenly, I stopped pacing and whirled around and . . . by George fell right over the edge of a little embankment . . . hadn't noticed it there before.

I climbed back out and gave him a steely gaze. "Are you ready to handle more responsibility?"

"Oh yeah, sure, you bet, unless . . . what's the job?"

I paced back over to him and, once again, placed my paw upon his shoulder. It was a touching moment.

"Drover, we're building up our profile of this cat and we need some additional information."

"And?"

"And we've selected you to . . . well, conduct a little survey, and ask the kitty a question. Here is the question: 'Kitty Cat, what would you say if I told you that I'm going to make sausage patties out of you?'"

He twisted his head and stared at me. "Sausage patties?"

"That's correct. It's just routine market research, Drover. We want to know what she thinks of . . . uh, sausage patties."

"Well, that sounds simple enough. Just ask her the question, huh?"

"Yes, and then come right back here and tell me her answer. I'll take it from there."

"Gosh, I can handle that. Here I go."

"Good luck, son."

While Drover went skipping around to the front of the cake house, I moved to a chinaberry grove nearby and established an observation post. There, I watched.

Very interesting. Her answer to the question about sausage patties was a handful of claws to Drover's nose. WHACK!! And instead of reporting back to me, the little mutt went screaming all the way back to the house.

Well, we had sustained a small blot on our

record, but we had gained important information. Mary D Cat wasn't one to waste words, and she had zero sense of humor. I mean zilch.

CHAPTER FIVE

We Teach the Cat
a Valuable Lesson
About Life

After entering all the info from the Drover Incident into my database, I drifted back to the cake house and watched Slim finish loading sacks of cake into the Cammo-Stealth.

And by the way, when I speak of "cake," I'm not talking about birthday cake or wedding cake or any of the other kinds of cake made with icing. Cake, in the ranchy sense of the word, is cow feed.

Cubes of feed, see, that are made out of compressed cottonseed. Ours was called "39% protein cottonseed cake," and it came in fifty-pound burlap sacks. We start feeding cake to the cows after the first frost, the reason being that after frost, the grass begins to lose its food value and the cows need some extra groceries to make it through the winter.

It's pretty impressive that a dog would know all that, isn't it?

On an ordinary day in the wintertime, Slim fed two pounds of cake per cow, but on this particular day, with the snow and everything, he decided to kick their grub up to three pounds.

We had two hundred cows on the Hodges' Place. If Slim was going to feed them three pounds per each, that meant . . . let's see here . . . we needed . . . hmm, how many sacks of feed? I'll have it worked out here in just a second . . . running a spreadsheet on . . . our hardware runs a little slow in this cold . . .

Okay, he loaded a bunch of sacks into the back of the Cammo-Stealth, and I really don't care how many. If you want to know the exact number, do the figgering yourself. I'm a very busy dog.

Where was I? Oh yes, watching Slim load up an undisclosed number of sacks into the so forth. Mary D Cat was watching too, but typical of her pattern of strange behavior, she wasn't content merely to watch. She had to get in the middle of things.

She hopped up into the cake house and Slim stumbled over her no less than three times. He booted her out the door every time, but that didn't seem to phase . . . phaze . . . fase . . . bother her at all. She went right back inside and rubbed on his legs.

Faize.

Then she hopped up on the stack of cake sacks, and when Slim stopped to catch his breath, she jumped onto his neck and started rubbing his ear. Now, that woke him up! I guess he thought a cobra had dropped down from the rafters, and when he felt that thing around his neck and heard that purring in his ear, he moved a little quicker than he was accustomed to moving.

Ran into the doorjamb, is what he did, and yelled. And when he saw that it was only the cat, he reached up and jerked her off his neck.

You know what a cat does when you try to jerk her off your neck? She digs in with her claws. Old Slim got her peeled off his neck but he paid a price for it. By then Kitty had worn out her welcome, and Slim drew back and tossed her as far as he could, through the air and into the snow.

I was standing nearby and watched her flight: ears up, tail straight out, and all four landing gears down. She looked like an . . . I don't know what. A flying squirrel. A falling star. A hairy, rocket-propelled something or other.

But it was very exciting to watch, and have I

mentioned that when cats make sudden movements like that, it gets me all stirred up? Yes, it's true, and it comes over me more or less on its own, without malice or forethought or much planning on my part.

There seems to be some mechanism in a dog's mind that makes him rush to the scene of a crashed cat and start barking, and that's what I did and . . . POW!

Sometimes that mechanism gets a dog into trouble before he knows it. I mean, I was just curious. Concerned. I hadn't actually intended to . . . that cat wasn't inclined to ask questions or take prisoners. At the first sign of trouble, she just loaded up and blasted away with her claws.

Yes, we took a few hits and sustained some damage to . . . well, lips, gums, cheeks, eyebrows, and the soft leathery portion of our nose, but that was a small price to pay for all the valuable intelligence information we gathered from the experience.

Yes, our file on Mary D Cat was growing larger and larger, and each new shred of evidence added to our profile of a sick and twisted mind. This latest incident certainly raised the possibility that this deranged cat didn't enjoy being barked at in close quarters.

Now, that's a sick mind. I mean, what possible harm . . . oh well. Now that we knew she would strike without warning, we fed this information into Data Control and got a new set of guidelines:

"So don't bark in her face."

Hm. I never would have thought of that, but by George, it seemed pretty good advice.

Just stop barking in her face.

Sure, okay. Good old Data Control.

Slim and Alfred climbed into the Cammo-Stealth, fired up the engine, and called for us dogs to load up in the back. I went flying into the back as gracefully as a deer and took the Scout Position on top of the spare tire.

Drover came out as far as the yard fence and stopped. I guess he saw the cat and didn't want to risk getting another faceful of her claws. Not a bad idea, actually. My nose was still throbbing. We had to pick him up in front of the house.

But the very second we puffed away from the cake house, here came Mary D Cat: "Wait, don't leave me! Take me away from here! Don't go! Cheese, I want some cheese! A friendly face!"

And get this. She came bounding up to the truck, leaped up on the running board, clawed her way up and ended up inside the cab on Slim's lap. He gave her the old heave-ho and away we went.

My ears flew up at this, which kicked in the voice of Data Control: *"So don't bark in her face."* Well, she was on the ground and well out of range, so I overrode DC and barked with all my heart and soul.

I love doing that. It's one of the pure joys of being a dog. It's where we discover the true meaning of Dogness.

We picked up Mister Scared-of-a-Wimpy-Little-Cat in front of the house and headed for the west pasture. Miss Kitty followed us for a ways, yowling.

"Meeee-yowwwwww! Meeeee-yowwww! Don't leave me, take me away from here, cheese, a friendly face!"

I moved to the back of the truck and gave her my final words. "It serves you right for being such a hateful little snot. Go catch a mouse, that's what you're here for, and always remember that Hank the Cowdog does not take trash off the cats!"

Even Drover got in on the deal. "Yeah, and me too! And now I'll bet you're sorry for being so mean."

"Well said, Drover."

"And I hope you get fleas and ringworms!"

"Oh, good shot, son, good shot! You really stuck her with that one." Grinning and barking and sticking out our tongues at her, we watched until she had disappeared in the distance. "Well,

Drover, we have notched up another victory over a cat."

"Yeah . . . I guess so. But she sure slapped the fire out of me."

"Don't worry about it, son. The important thing here is that, once again, superior dog intelligence has triumphed over the forces of Kittydom."

He rubbed a bloody spot on his nose and I, well, rubbed a bloody spot on my nose—caused, no doubt, by the dangerous cockleburs.

Yes, of course. That had to be it.

"I wonder what got her so worked up," said Drover. "All I did was ask her about sausage patties, and she didn't even answer."

"I can't imagine, Drover."

"She just hauled off and slugged me."

"I'll swan."

"I guess she doesn't like sausage."

"Don't try to find intelligent reasons for the behavior of a cat, Drover. They're all nutty, and that one is even nuttier than most. Just forget about it. It's water under the dam."

We turned our attention to more important matters, such as the feed run and the snowstorm. And making it up that long steep hill west of the house.

The road was slick and covered with snow,

don't you see, and making it up that long steep hill would have been no easy deal even in dry weather. But that's why we had switched over to the Cammo-Stealth, right?

Up front, Slim and Little Alfred were having a good time. Slim threw the truck into four-wheel drive and first gear, and we hit the hill with a good head of steam. And let me tell you, fellers, the old Cammo-Stealth just ATE that hill.

The engine roared and threw mud with all four wheels, and above it all, I could hear Little Alfred making truck sounds of his own.

"Ud-un, ud-un, ud-un! Rrrrrrrrrrummmmmmmm!"

I was up in the Scout Position again, checking out the country ahead and letting the wind blow my ears around. Say, this was fun! What more could a ranch dog ask of life? This was true cow-dog happiness.

It was then that I caught sight of two brown shadows that darted across the road in front of us. Could they be . . . yes, they were coyotes, perhaps two brothers I had known in bygone days?

They stopped in some bushes on the left side of the road, and as we roared past them, I got a good look at their faces. And yes, it was Rip and Snort.

Well, I was feeling rather expansive and full of myself, you might say, I being motorized and they

being afoot. And perhaps I said a few things that would have been better left unsaid. You know how it is when you pass some guys walking. Sometimes you just can't resist the temptation to mouth off.

And I did. Mouth off, that is, not resist the temptation.

"Hey, you guys need a ride? Ha, ha, call a taxi! Too bad you don't have a Cammo-Stealth army truck to ride around in." I stuck my tongue out at them. "There, take that! And furthermore, your momma wears gunnysack underpants!"

Yes, perhaps it was a little childish, but it was also FUN, and there's more to this life than work and worry. A guy has to have a little fun now and then, even if he's Head of Ranch Security.

There was only one little problem with this interlude of fun. At that very moment, Slim made a hard left turn and . . .

Something very bad happened.

CHAPTER SIX

The Very Bad "Something" That Happened

Here's what happened:

I had moved my business from the spare tire to a position near the back of the truck bed, in order to make my communication with the coyote brothers somewhat easier, don't you see, and I sure wasn't expecting Slim to jerk the truck hard to the left.

But he did and suddenly I found myself hung out to dry, you might say. The truck went left and I went right—over the side and into a snowbank, which wasn't too funny, since I had just been mouthing off to . . .

Yikes! Slim was speeding up, shifting gears, driving away!

47

"Hey, wait a minute, what about me! Drover, don't just sit there. Do something!"

He was running in circles in the back of the truck. "Oh my gosh, Hank fell out, stop, murder, oh my leg!"

I chased them for a hundred yards or so and gave up. Slim never looked back, never saw a thing. He must have been yakking to Little Alfred. Or singing. He often sings when he's feeding cattle.

Oh well, the situation wasn't really as serious as I had first thought. Yes, it was a little scary to get dumped out in the middle of that wild canyon country, but Slim still had two more pastures to feed before he headed back to Wolf Creek.

When he got out to feed the cows in the Picket Canyon pasture, he would notice the huge silence and vacancy created by my absence.

No doubt he would gasp and recoil in horror, and say something like, "Holy smokes, I've lost my dog, and that dog's worth hundreds and thousands of dollars. No, he's priceless. You can't put a price on a dog like Hank."

True, very true.

And then he would say, "I can't believe I was so careless with the Head of Ranch Security. I should have let him ride up front, but I didn't, and I could kick myself for taking chances with a dog that's worth more than gold or silver."

Exactly. Or diamonds or rubies, for that matter.

"Well, I'll just have to backtrack until I find him. We can't go home until we find our Hank."

Right, because if he did, Little Alfred would be heartbroken. Loper would be furious. Sally May would be . . . well, we needn't speculate on that, but I was pretty sure that she would be upset.

It would all work out. I would just hike back to the house and wait for the crew to come looking for me. Then we could all have a joyous reunion and laugh about it—although I would have to give Slim a few hurtful looks, so as not to let him completely off the hook.

It WAS pretty careless of him to throw me out of the truck, as he himself had admitted.

I trotted up the hill, thinking that when I reached the crest, I would look down into the valley and see the Cammo-Stealth streaking back to find me.

I reached the top of the hill and stopped for a breather. I looked off to the west and saw . . . hmm, lot of snow. Oh well, it would take 'em a while to discover the tragedy. A guy just had to give 'em a little time.

I walked across the cattle guard and started

down the hill, and noticed . . . dog tracks in the snow? Hmm, that was interesting. Had I walked down this hill earlier in the day? No. Had Drover? No.

Hmmm. Then apparently we had some stray dogs on the place, and you know where I stand on the issue of stray dogs. I don't . . .

Coyote tracks?

Suddenly I remembered my passing remarks to the coyote brothers, something about their mother wearing . . . what was it? Gunnysack undergarments?

I, uh, suddenly became aware of the fact that I was walking down the middle of the road, exposed for all the world to see. Very shortly after this thought occurred to me, I found myself creeping through the taller forms of vegetation in the vicinity, such as the clumps of little bluestem grass, Indian grass, skunkbrush, mountain mahogany, and wild plum thickets.

No, I certainly didn't need another encounter with those guys. I'd learned just about all I needed to know about cannibal life . . . and there they were!

Fifty yards ahead of me and I almost had a heart attack. I stopped in my tracks and sank down to my belly and watched them through the little bluestem—which, by the way, was a reddish-brown color, not blue or even close to blue, so why did they call it bluestem?

Not that I cared, you understand, because I had bigger problems on my hands. I watched them through the grass. They trotted across the road some fifty yards ahead of me. I could hear them laughing and belching, which is fairly typical behavior for happy cannibals.

Lucky for me, the wind was coming straight

out of the north, so it carried my scent away from them. Otherwise, I might have been a cooked goose, because those guys have noses like you won't believe.

They crossed the road, just about where we had seen them earlier, and disappeared up a short deep canyon to the north. I waited for a long time, just to be sure they had gone. Then I switched over to Ultra-Crypto Creeping Mode and moved out on silent paws.

I hadn't gone more than a hundred yards when . . . holy smokes, a branch snapped and I whirled around to face . . .

Okay, the wind had caused a branch to creak in a hackberry tree to my right and that was no big deal, but I had enjoyed about all of that creeping I could stand, and I went to Full Throttle on all engines and zoomed the rest of the way back to the camp house.

It would have been very nice, very satisfying if I had found the truck there waiting for me. That would have closed out the day on a happy note. But the truck was not there.

Instead of being greeted by Slim and all my old friends, I was greeted by this . . . this long-haired yowling thing that came bounding out of the yard.

"A crust of bread? Baloney, cheese?
Spare a morsel, if you please.
Marooned, I am, oh hateful place!
At last I've found a friendly face!"

Would you care to guess what she did immediately? She started rubbing on me, of course, and babbling.

"Did you happen to bring some cheese? Just a little bite would be fine. I crave cheese, I dream of cheese, and maybe you could take me away from here. I've been marooned these two long years."

I backed away from her. "No, I don't have any cheese. And no, I can't take you away from here."

She followed me and continued to rub and purr. "You'll stay a while, won't you? We have so much to talk about."

"I'd love to sit and talk, Kitty, but I'm afraid I won't be here that long. My ride will be arriving any minute now, and we'll have to say *hors d'oeuvre* until another day."

I backed up another three steps. She followed. "Where there's an *hors d'oeuvre,* there's a piece of cheese."

"Uh, no. I'm afraid you've missed the translation. *Hors d'oeuvre* is French for 'good-bye.' I speak many languages, you see, including French,

Italian, Thousand Island, and Ranch, so I have many ways of saying good-bye."

"Don't say good-bye. You just got here and we haven't talked."

"Yes, and I can't tell you how much I regret that, because I don't regret it." I trotted away from her again. "We haven't talked and we never will talk. In the first place, you're a cat and I make it a habit not to talk with cats."

Here she came again. I kept moving.

"Talking with cats is not only a waste of time, but it's also a violation of the Cowdog Code. We're not allowed to mingle with cats on the job. Or off the job. Or anywhere else. Nothing personal, but you're a cat.

"In the second place, my ride will be here any minute now." I stopped and scanned the horizon in all directions. Nothing. Not a sound except the soft tinkle of snowflakes. "My business associates will be picking me up soon and . . ."

She had caught up with me. I crawled under a barbed wire fence and trotted out into the horse pasture.

"And in the third place . . . I hate to put it this way, Kitty, but you are absolutely driving me nuts with all that rubbing and purring!"

"But I haven't seen a friendly face in so long!"

"Yes, and it's made you a lunatic. That's what you are, a lunatic cat, and nobody could stand to be around you for more than a minute."

All at once her whole manner changed. Her eyes widened. Her jaw began to tremble. Tears slid down her cheeks. "You called me a lunatic cat!"

"Yes ma'am, I did."

"You don't care about me."

"Yes ma'am, that's correct. In my deepest heart of hearts, I think you are totally weird."

She burst out crying. "Nobody loves me, everybody hates me, I'm going to eat some worms!"

And with that, she went flying back into the yard, crawled under the house through a hole in the foundation, and disappeared. In the silence, I could hear her sobbing under the house.

Well, it served her right.

CHAPTER SEVEN

Holy Smokes, I've Been Abandoned!

I returned to the front of the house and began pacing around near the point where three pasture trails merged with the main road out of the ranch.

Slim would be coming down one of those roads and I wanted to be there when he came through. I was pretty sure that he would stop anyway, and honk his horn and call for me, because . . . well, by then he would have missed me and would be frantic with concern, but I didn't want to take any chances on getting left.

So I paced around in the middle of the road—waiting, watching, listening. In the course of listening, what I heard was Mary D Cat, crying under the house.

It didn't bother me at all, even though we Heads of Ranch Security have a warm side to our nature and we are famous for being kind to children. I mean, that's just bred into us. To become a Head of Ranch Security, a guy must take a Solemn Cowdog Oath to protect and defend and be nice to all children, even the ones who are bratty.

But we also have this other side, which is cold and hard and made of quarter-inch-steel armored plate. It allows us to conduct slashing interrogations and solve murder cases without the slightest quiver of emotion. We're talking about your basic hard-boiled ranch dog here, and listening to sad stories is just part of the job.

It was this cold, hard side of my nature that greeted the sobs of Mary D Cat. Yes, I heard them but they bounced off my steel-plated eardrums like . . . I don't know what, but they bounced off.

I continued to pace in the snow.

Don't get me wrong. Making ladies cry had never been high on my list of Fun Things to Do, even lady cats. Maybe some dogs get a kick out of it but I don't. I do it when I have to. It just goes with the job.

Every once in a while you make a lady cry. It can't be helped, and I wished she would stop crying.

Hey, I'd told the truth, is all. If she couldn't handle the truth, that was her problem.

I had problems of my own.

What was keeping Slim so long? I cocked my ear and listened. Crying. Weeping. Sobbing.

The only thing more annoying than a cat that rubs is one that crawls under a house and cries. I have absolutely no use for . . .

I changed the direction of my pacing, ever so slightly, and eased over to a point in front of the house. "Kitty, you can't help it that you're weird. You do the best you can with what you have, which isn't much."

More blubbering.

"Look, everyone in this world has to be something, and you happen to be a little crazy. It's no big deal."

More blubbering.

I slipped under the fence and stood in front of the hole in the foundation.

"I wish you wouldn't do that. I mean, you can't just fall apart when somebody tells you the truth. I gave you my honest opinion, what more can I say?" No change. "Look, will you say something? I'll be leaving soon and . . ."

I stuck my head into the hole. I couldn't see her in the darkness but I could hear her, loud and clear.

"Look, my car and driver will be here any minute now. I'm a very busy dog and I don't have time to waste on crybabies and bawl-bags."

At last she spoke—through tears, of course. "I'm not a crybaby or a bawl-bag! I'm just a poor lonely cat who's been marooned for two long years and wants a bite of cheese and a friend. But nobody cares."

"Yes, that's sort of the bottom line, isn't it? Well, I'm going to be leaving here in a minute, so let's try

to wrap this deal up. I'll be coming back to feed the cows another day. You work on your problems and get all the tears out of your system and maybe we can sit down and talk about it. What do you say to that?"

She said . . . more tears.

"Look, cat, do you want to resolve this thing or not? I don't have all day. My ride will . . ." Just then I heard the hum of a motor. "Well, there's my ride. I have to go. Have a great day." She bawled louder at that. "Well, what do you want me to say? Have an awful day? Okay, have an awful day. Adios, good-bye, and *hors d'oeuvre.*"

Too bad for her I had done my best. I wiggled my way out of the hole—I had gotten myself a little farther under the house than I had planned—I wiggled my way out of the hole, put Miss Mary D Cat and her problems behind me, and . . .

. . . saw the Cammo-Stealth army truck go down the road and disappear behind a curtain of snow.

Hey, wait a minute! Why didn't he stop or blow his horn? How was I supposed to . . . I'd been waiting out there in the middle of the road!

I went dashing away from the house and down the road. I barked. I yelled. I went to Turbo-Lightning Speed and chased the truck half a mile, until my Turbo-Lightning turned to Turbo-Mush. Exhausted, I stopped.

And there, standing in the middle of the road, in the silence, with snowflakes falling on my nose, I had to face the awful truth. Slim hadn't even noticed that I was missing. He had left me and I was now marooned and abandoned, a dog without a home or a country.

And for some reason, I found myself thinking about . . . cheese.

CHEESE?

That was ridiculous, totally absurd. I didn't even like cheese. It was too hard to chew and it gummed up my teeth, hence, it followed from simple logic that I would not allow myself to think about it.

Hey, I not only didn't like cheese but I knew that craving cheese was one of the first symptoms of it was worse than fleas or ringworm and I didn't want it and I would NOT allow myself to become a victim of Cheesarosis.

No way. That was all right for weirdo crybaby cats, but not for dogs.

Furthermore, just because I was now marooned and abandoned didn't mean that I was going to rush back to the house and establish diplomatic relations with Mary D Cat. No thanks.

In the first place, there was a very high probability that Slim would discover his error and come streaking back to the canyon country to rescue me. Hence, my period of exile would probably not last long.

A couple of hours at the most. Nothing to be alarmed about. In fact, at that very moment I turned and looked down the road . . . and didn't see him coming.

But then again, I really hadn't, uh, expected him back so soon anyways, so no big deal there.

In the second place, I had always considered myself a very self-sufficient dog, the kind of dog who enjoyed his own company and could always find ways of passing the time.

Now, your ordinary dogs—your poodles, your house dogs, your little yip-yips—they couldn't spend a minute alone without going into a panic. Why? Because they are such boring little mutts that to spend time alone with them is to die a slow, boring death.

Not me, fellers. When I'm alone, I'm in the company of the most interesting and resourceful dog I know, so the thought of being marooned with ME for an hour or two, or half a day, or a whole day or even several days or a week . . .

Gulp.

Okay, maybe it wouldn't be all that great, but I knew that I could handle it.

Self-discipline, that's the secret, and I had gobs of self-discipline. And I sure as thunder didn't crave the company of a sniveling piece of cheese.

The company of a cat, I should say. A sniveling cat.

And I didn't go streaking back to the house. I *walked* back to the house. And did I go straight to the hole in the foundation and tell my sad story to Mary D Cat? No sir, I did not. I established a temporary camp in the middle of the road and didn't even get close to the cheese.

Close to the house, I should say, didn't even get close to the house. No, I dug myself a little bed in the snow, right in the middle of the road where Slim could find me when he came roaring back . . .

He would be so embarrassed and angry with himself. And apologetic. Imagine, him leaving his Head of Ranch Security at the Hodges' Place! He would beg for understanding and forgiveness. I would grant it, but not right away

These wounds take time to heal.

And I wanted him to learn his lesson from it.

I curled up in the snow and watched the snowflakes fall and kept my eyes locked on the point where the road disappeared into the soft curtain of cheese.

Of snow, I should say.

The point is that I was self-sufficient and perfectly content to spend a couple of hours by myself, thinking deep thoughts and laughing at my own wit, and the hours dragged by and I thought I would go nuts.

Where were they! Why hadn't they come streaking back to save me from this horrible silence and isolation? Hey, darkness was falling across the canyon and the coyotes were howling, and there I was, marooned and exiled and abandoned, and I wanted . . .

I wanted some cheese!

And suddenly it occurred to me that Mary D Cat, uh, needed a friend.

Someone to listen to her sad tale of woe.

A shoulder to cry on.

And, what the heck, I had a few minutes to burn, so I, uh, hiked over to the house and looked her up.

CHAPTER EIGHT

The Cat Insists on Being My Friend and Ally

I wandered over to the hole in the foundation and glanced over both shoulders to make sure that no one was watching. No one was, of course, I knew that. But still, this was embarrassing.

I pointed my nose toward the hole. "Uhhhhh, Miss Mary D? Hello? Are you still there? I've experienced a slight change in plans. Maybe you should come out so we can talk about it."

I could hear her sniffling under there, but for a long time she didn't answer. Then I heard her voice. "No, I won't come out. You said I was weird."

"Perhaps you have me confused with someone else, ma'am. I'm almost sure I wouldn't have said such a thing, and if you'll just come out, we can . . ."

"You said it. I heard you. You said I was a weird cat and nobody cared about me."

"No, no, I think what we have here is a simple case of mistaken identity. You're probably thinking of my companion, my friend, Drover— small sawed-off, stub-tailed little mutt. I often get blamed for his, uh, careless remarks, don't you see."

"It was you, and I'm not coming out."

I took a deep breath and glanced around. It was getting dark. "Okay, maybe it was me. I admit it. Did you hear that?"

"Keep going."

"I, well, there isn't much more to say, really. I admit that I was misquoted and I accept full and total responsibility for everything that happened . . . although I still say you shouldn't have taken it so hard."

"Are you sorry for making me cry?"

"I, uh . . . am I sorry for . . . ? Okay, okay, let's get it over with. I made a few careless remarks and I'm sorry they hurt your feelings and made you cry . . . although I must add . . ."

"You'd better stop while you're ahead, doggie."

I glared at the dark hole from whence her voice came. "Yes ma'am, I guess you're right. Now, will you please come out?"

She came out and looked at me with a pair of sad, red-rimmed eyes. "What are you doing here? I thought you were leaving."

"Yes, exactly. I, too, thought I was leaving, but instead of leaving, I got left."

Her eyes brightened on that. "Ohhhhh, how exciting! You mean we're marooned together?"

"That seems to be the case, and let's get right to the . . . you, uh, don't happen to have some cheese, do you? All at once I have this powerful craving for cheese, and I don't even like the stuff."

She began purring and rubbing on my leg. "I know. It must have something to do with being marooned. With me, it started the first day, and I've been hungry for cheese for two years. Weird, isn't it?"

"Yes, it's weird and it's not like me at all, and let's go straight to the bottom line, ma'am. Circumstances have placed us on the same team, so to speak."

"Oh? You want my help, is that what you're saying?"

"I, uh . . . I'm not one who needs help very often or who enjoys asking for it, but yes, I seem

68

to be . . ." I coughed. "I seem to find myself . . ."
This was very painful. "We appear to have reached
the point where I need your help, yes."

"Otherwise, you might not survive the night?"

"That's, uh . . . that thought had occurred to
me, yes. And a guy doesn't need to worry about
the second night until he's survived the first one,
is sort of how it looks from here."

"Yes, the coyotes are bad in these canyons,
and the bobcats are even worse. Do you want my
advice?"

"No, actually I thought . . ." I swallowed hard.
"Yes, I want your advice. After all, you're the one
who's stayed alive down here for two years."

"That's right." She kept on rubbing on my leg.
"I'd advise you to spend the night under the house.
It's the only safe place on the ranch."

I moved several steps away from her. "Yes,
right. I had already reached that same conclusion
myself."

"There's only one problem, doggie."

"You can call me Hank, and what's the problem?"

"You don't like cats."

"I don't like . . . ha, ha, ha. Whatever gave you
that idea? I mean . . . okay, it's sort of natural for
cats and dogs to be on opposite sides, but I think

that we, uh, have room for compromise here, given the unusual circumstances and so forth."

"You don't think you'd mind staying under the house with a cat?"

"I feel that we can . . . work around that, yes. No problem."

"But there's still another problem. I rub on things, and you don't like that."

She came over and rubbed me on the front legs, rubbed my left side, my tail section, and then my right side. I sat there as still as a statue, fighting against all my natural impulses to make fangs and growl.

Fellers, this was one of the toughest assignments of my whole career. All my years of Security Work rose up inside my head and called for me to snarl and snap at that cat. But I sat there and took it. I had no choice.

"Actually, ma'am, I'm discovering a whole new appreciation for the, uh, rubbing process. There's something soothing about it and . . ." And I wanted to bite her tail in half SO BADLY! "The rubbing business might be a small problem, especially at first, but the alternatives are not all that great. In other words, I think we can work that one out too."

"Well, I'd hate for you to be unhappy."

"Oh no. No, no. I'm very, uh, happy. Very." And

if she didn't quit rubbing on me and flicking that
tail across my nose, I was going to ...

Just then, I heard coyotes howling in the distance. "No sir, that rubbing will be no problem
whatever. You just rub all you want and, by George,
we'll ... do you suppose we ought to finish this conversation under the house?"

"Yes, I guess we should. I'd rather stay outside
and enjoy the fresh air, but it starts getting dangerous at this time of night."

I headed for the hole in the foundation. "Right, so why don't we just head for the fort?"

"Sometimes the coyotes come right up to the opening and bark at me. They like to eat cats, you know."

"Yes, and guard dogs too. I've had a little experience with those guys, and it makes sleeping under the house sound pretty good to me."

I waited for her to go under the house—ladies first, you know—and I followed, wiggling my way through the narrow space between the ground and the floor of the house. It wasn't so easy for me to get around in such tight quarters, I mean, with my huge thighs and massive shoulders and everything, but I had pretty strong incentive to make it work.

We crawled all the way to the northwest corner, as far away from the opening as we could get. It was very dark in there and also dusty, but I was learning to like it.

I still couldn't believe Slim had left me down there. What a lousy way to treat the Head of Ranch Security! Well, if I could just make it through one night with the cat, surely he'd be back to get me the next day.

Although . . . oops, he was feeding the Hodges' Place every other day, not every day, which meant . . . what if nobody missed me at all? That was hard for me to believe, but stranger things had happened in the world.

Well, there we were, and Madame Kitty was having the time of her life, rubbing and purring, purring and rubbing and dragging her tail across my face. After all those months and years of being alone, she had something warm to rub on, and before she got done with me, I would probably be as bald as a Thanksgiving turkey.

I hated it. Every second seemed like a minute, and every minute seemed like an hour. Would this go on all night? Didn't she ever sleep?

Well, maybe she didn't sleep at night, but I certainly did. Sleeping happened to be one of the things I did particularly well, and it didn't take me long to drift off and start pushing up a long line of Z's.

Zzzzzzzzzzzzzzzzzzzzzzzzzzzzzzzzzzzzzzzzzzzzzzzz.

As you might expect, I dreamed of the lovely, incomparable Miss Beulah the Collie. Who would want to dream of anyone else? I had gone visiting at her place and we were sitting together in the shade of that big native elm north of the house. Plato, the spotted dumb-bunny bird dog, was nowhere in sight, which pleased me very much.

In real life he was always around, like flies

and gnats, but this was my dream, and in my dreams we have no bird dogs. Who needs 'em? And why Miss Beulah continued to waste her time hanging around that . . . oh well.

I am still the master of my dreams, and in my dreams we have zero bird dogs.

There we were, Miss Beulah and I, sitting in the . . . I've already said that. I cocked my head to a rakish angle and said in my smoothest voice, "Well, my prairie winecup, here we are, alone at last. A penny for your thoughts."

She gave me that secret smile that sent little shock waves all the way out to the end of my tail. And then she leaned toward me, so that I caught the scent of her aroma, and said, "Cheese. Would you like some cheese?"

"Well I . . . yes. Those aren't exactly the thoughts I had expected to buy for a penny, but yes, I would love some cheese."

And then—you won't believe this—then she rolled in a huge wheel of cheese. I mean, that thing must have been five feet across, and we started gobbling cheese in big bites and I found myself talking with my mouth full.

"Well Beulah, let's talk about love, shall we?"

"Yes, let's. I love cheese."

"Mmmm, yes, and so do I. And you know what,

Beulah? I used to think only of you, but now I think only of cheese. Love is crazy, isn't it, my dear?"

"Yes," she said with her mouth stuffed with cheese, "and love is blond, the same color as cheese. Oh Hank, this is so romantic, talking to each other with our mouths stuffed with cheese!"

"Yes, my love, and blowing cheese crumbs in each other's faces. This is the way I'd always hoped it would be."

Well, it was a beautiful dream, but just then, guess who walked up and ruined it all. You'll never guess.

CHAPTER NINE

Hint: His Name Was Leroy

Y ou probably guessed Plato the Bird Dog, right? No, absolutely wrong.

Well, not absolutely wrong. It was partly wrong and partly right, and let me explain.

In the dream, Beulah and I were there alone, sitting under the tree, and we've already covered that two or three times, when out of nowhere, who should appear but Mister Bird Watcher himself.

Well, I wasn't about to let Plato ruin another precious encounter with my one and only true love in the whole world—cheese. (I know this sounds odd but dreams are that way sometimes.) Anyways, he came blundering into the middle of this precious romantic encounter, and as you might expect, he wanted some of our cheese.

I told him to buzz off, but instead of buzzing off, he went to the giant wheel of cheese, opened his jaws, and was about to snap off a big bite— only he didn't get the chance because I, tee hee, clubbed him over the head with my enormous paw.

That would teach him a valuable lesson about . . . hmmmmm, that was odd. I seemed to be picking up the smell of skunk. It was very faint at first, but it didn't stay faint for long. In fact, it became so strong that I almost fainted.

And . . . holy smokes, that's when the dream rolled away and I found myself back in the real world, under the house at the Hodges' Place. And I was staring straight into the hateful little eyes of a . . . skunk?

Yes, indeed. In my dream, I had thought he was Plato and I had bopped him on the nose, and that had been exactly the wrong thing to do.

Have we discussed skunks? They often take up residence under ranch houses, don't you see, and Mary D Cat had neglected to tell me that she was sharing the place with a loaded stink bomb, and the last thing you want to do to a loaded skunk under the house is to heckle him or get him stirred up with provocatory gestures.

Suddenly my eyes were burning and my lungs

were burning. All the circuits on the Smellatory
Panel hit "Overload" and sirens began going off
in my head. I couldn't breathe, I could hardly see,
my instrumentation was blown. Smoke and fire
and flames filled the control room, and my whole
life had come down to two words: Fresh air!

I staggered and stumbled through the darkness, ran into water pipes and conked my head on
floor joists and cinder-block piers, fought my way
through the green poisonous air, until at last I
reached the escape hatch and tumbled out into
the sweet cold air of night.

Gasping for breath, I looked around and saw
Mary D standing a few feet away. She was licking

her paw. "I should have known that you and Leroy wouldn't get along."

"Leroy!" I gasped. "You mean he has a name?"

"Oh sure. We share the place. He stays on his side and I stay on mine. He's okay with cats but you must have said something that really hurt his feelings. I mean, he's never done this before."

"I didn't say anything. I was having this dream, see, and I thought . . . never mind, it's too complicated. The bottom line is that I punched him."

She stared at me and shook her head. "Uh, uh, uh. You should never punch Leroy."

"I realize that."

"I wish you hadn't done it."

I pushed myself up on all fours. "Well, I kind of regret it myself, and I'm sorry you didn't tell me that I was moving into a den of skunks."

"Leroy's the only one and he's really a nice guy."

"I noticed."

"You just can't punch him around."

"Hey, it was an accident, and could we change the subject? Such as, what do we do now?"

She cranked up her purring machine and started rubbing on me again. "Well, I'm afraid we've lost the house. This has never happened to me before and . . ."

Suddenly, her eyes turned into flaming circles of fire. She humped her back and started hissing, like a . . . I don't know what. A cobra, I guess, a hissing, angry cobra that had gone insane. And she drew back her right paw and aimed a handful of sharp claws at my nose.

Lucky for me, I saw it coming and used my lightning-fast reflexes to dodge the punch, otherwise . . . hmmm, otherwise our friendship might have ended there, and she might have . . .

Anyways, she humped up and hissed and threw a wild punch, and then she started screeching at me.

"You bozo, I offered to help you and took you in to save your stupid skin, and look what you've done!"

"It was an accident."

"Accident! Is that all you can say? You found the only skunk within five miles of here and punched him out!"

"I was dreaming."

"Dreaming! Is that all you can say? You've ruined my friendship with Leroy!"

"I thought he was a bird dog."

"Bird dog! Is that all you can say?"

"What do you want me to say?"

"I want you to say . . ." Suddenly her screech

changed into a moan, and she burst out crying again. "I want you to take me away from here! My home is wrecked. It's all I had to show for two long lonely years. I have no place to hide. The coyotes will eat me. Oh Homer, take me away from here!"

"My name is Hank, actually."

Her head came up, and once again her eyes were aflame. "Do I care what your name is? You've ruined my life, you clam-brain, and now you'd better get me out of here!"

"Don't screech at me."

"I'll screech at you! I'll tear out your eyeballs!"

"Okay, screech all you want."

She went back to tears. "Is that all you can say? I've just lost my home and now you ask me to screech about it? What kind of heartless brute are you?"

Oh boy. I walked a few steps away and waited for her to get control of herself. At last she did. She came up behind me.

"Homer, our situation is serious. We'll be sitting ducks for the predators if we stay here."

"I agree. If you can get us out of these canyons, I can find the way back to my ranch."

"I know a trail out of the canyon. It will take us up on top, but it will be dangerous."

I looked down at her. "Well, it appears to me that anything we do around here will be dangerous. Trying to carry on a normal conversation with you is dangerous. Every five minutes, you're wanting to tear out my eyeballs."

"I've been down here too long. It's made me weird."

"When I told you that, you threw a fit."

She shrugged. "Cats are that way."

"I told you *that,* too, and you threw another fit. And my name's not Homer. It's Hank."

"Well, my name's not Kitty. It's Mary D Cat."

"I like Kitty better."

"I like Homer better."

"Hmm, well . . . this is all very interesting, but I guess we'd better get out of here. Which way is out?"

"Follow me."

She headed north, through the corrals and beyond, into the deep forbidding darkness of Picket Canyon. That place was pretty scary, even in the light of day, but at night . . .

Although I had some hesitations and reservations about following a cat anywhere, I did lower my standards to the point of allowing Mary D Cat to lead our group out of the canyon. And stayed pretty close to her, as a matter of fact.

We had gone about half a mile when we topped

a little hill near the place where the trail splits, and the left fork goes over to Scott Springs. The main trail, if you remember, goes on up the canyon to Moonshine Springs.

Or maybe you don't remember, if you've never been there. And maybe you haven't been there. But it does.

Anyways, the cat stopped on that little hill and looked back to the south. She heaved a deep sigh and shook her head.

"I just can't do it."

"You just can't do *what*?"

"Leave."

I stared at her in utter, complete disbelief. "What do you mean, you can't leave? That's all you've been talking about since the first minute I met you—'Take me away from here, get me away from this ranch!'"

Once again she was—I couldn't believe this, just couldn't believe it—she was crying again! "I know, but it's still my home. How can I leave the place that's been my home for two years?"

"Easy. You just keep walking."

"But I can't walk away from all the memories: the sun coming up over the caprock, the wild-flowers in the springtime, the mesas sinking into purple shadows at sunset."

I'd had just about enough. I stuck my nose in her face and growled. "Look, cat, you're my ticket out of here. Never mind the memories. Start walking or we're going to have us a little riot."

She humped up and hissed, and her eyes took on that same crazy look I'd seen so many times before.

"Listen, bozo, don't you tell ME what to do or I'll tear out your eyeballs!"

I don't know what might have happened if the coyotes hadn't appeared just then, but they did and we never had a chance to find out.

Did they devour both of us right there in one big cannibal feast? You'll just have to read on and see.

CHAPTER TEN

I Can't Believe
I Decided
to Help a Cat

Okay, I had gone nose-to-nose with the cat, when all at once I saw a pair of big yellow eyes looking at me.

And they weren't Mary D Cat's eyes. That gave me my first clue that they belonged to someone else, and I couldn't think of anyone else I wanted to meet in that canyon on a dark night.

Then a second pair of eyes appeared. That gave me my second clue that they belonged to someone else. Mary D had only one pair of eyes, don't you see.

"Kitty," I said in a low voice, "I'm afraid we've been found by the coyotes. You're the survival expert around here. What do we do now?"

I couldn't believe what she said. "Well, it's all over. We're finished."

"What do you mean, *we're finished!* What about all your survival tricks? What about tearing out their eyeballs?"

She gave me a sad smile. "That was just a bluff. It works on dogs but not on coyotes. Nothing works on coyotes. I'm a dead cat, Harvey, and nothing can save me."

"Yeah, but . . . what about . . ."

She shook her head. "It's no use. I always knew they'd get me, and they did. But you can make a run for it. They won't follow you."

"Me make a . . . that wouldn't be a very noble thing to do."

"No, but who needs to be noble at a time like this?"

"Hmm. That's a point. And you're just a cat. The world is full of cats."

"That's right. Only one Me but plenty of cats."

I began easing off to the north. "Well, Mary D, it was a real pleasure meeting you. I have mixed feelings about running out on you like this, but I think I can live with my feelings."

She waved a paw. "Go north until you come to Moonshine Springs. Just west of the spring, you'll find a trail out of the canyon. I'll stall them as long as I can. Good-bye, Harvey. When you get back to civilization, eat a piece of cheese for Mary D Cat."

"I sure will, and thanks for . . ."

"Go! Hurry!"

Since the coyotes were almost upon us, that seemed good advice. I turned and made a lightning dash up the canyon. Free at last! Boy, that had been a close call. Why, if the cat hadn't . . .

I couldn't believe she'd done that. It was almost enough to force me to rethink my Position on Cats. I mean, I'd always thought of cats as selfish and . . .

I found myself slowing to a walk. It just wasn't right—me walking away from danger and leaving a poor helpless cat to be mauled by cannibals. I mean, I'd had some success in dealing with coyotes before, and maybe I could . . .

You won't believe this, but I found myself reversing directions and heading back down the canyon. I couldn't believe it either. I mean, she was only a CAT and the world was full of cats and who cared if . . .

When I arrived back at the scene, the coyote brothers were standing over Mary D. They were licking their chops. They seemed fairly surprised at my sudden appearance.

"Evening, guys, how's it going? Hey, you found

my cat, thanks a million. I'd love to stay and talk,
but we're kind of in a hurry, don't you see, and . .

The brothers glanced at each other and sta ͭᵉᵈ
laughing. "Ha! Hunk big stupid for blun ͭ ᵗ into
coyote camp!"

"Stupid? Hey, I didn't blunder in ͪ ᵉ· I came
to pick up my cat."

They got a bigger laugh ou that. "Ha,
plenty stupid, 'cause coyote no ᵉ up cat, and
not give up Hunk, too, 'caus ͫ ᵘⁿᵏ same guy

who made foolish talk from back of truck—about coyote momma."

"That? Hey, that was nothing, just a little joke, guys. Honest."

"Uh! little joke on Hunk, 'cause Hunk now stay for big coyote feast, oh boy!"

I had sort of expected this. I mean, I really hadn't expected them to let us walk away without an argument, and it just so happened that I had prepared a clever plan.

It was a very clever plan and I knew it would work, because I had tried it several times before and it had never failed. The plan rested on my knowledge of the coyote mind. I knew how they thought, see, and I knew their weak spots. Watch this.

I waited for them to stop laughing at their good fortune. Then, "You know, Snort, I happen to be familiar with your culture and tradition, and I know that before a major feast, you guys love to fight and gamble and sing."

Snort shook his head. "Eat first. Then sing and grumble and fight and sing."

"No, you've got it backwards. The singing and gambling come first, because after a big meal, you like to take nap."

They whispered back and forth. Then Snort said, "Maybe Coyote like big nap."

"Right. And as I recall, you guys think you're pretty hot-rod singers."

"Not thinking. Knowing for sure. Coyote berry hop-rod singers, berriest hop-rod singers in whole world."

I gave them a careless chuckle. "Yeah, well, that's what I'm leading up to. It's been a while since we went up against each other in a major singing contest, and it happens that I've got a new song that will just blow your drawers off."

Snort scowled. "Uh. Coyote not wear drawers."

"Well, you know what I mean. My song is so good, I'm sure it would beat any song you guys could come up with—that is, if you can come up with a song."

"Huh! Coyote got plenty song. Coyote berry better singest in whole world."

"An idle boast, Snort, unless you're willing to try it out in a contest that's fair and square."

The brothers shook their heads. "Coyote not give a hoot for fair and square. Coyote like to cheat."

"I know, Snort, but this contest must be fair and square, for you see, if I win the Battle of the Songs, you must let me and my cat go free."

"Sound pretty crazy."

"Right, but you guys are pretty crazy, too."

"Uh. Coyote pretty crazy, all right."

"See? We agree on everything, and just to make sure that the contest is fair and square, I'm going to be the judge because . . . well, everyone knows that I'm, uh, fair and square and impartial. Honest. No kidding. I really am."

The brothers held a conference and talked it over. Then Snort said, "Coyote not care who judge contest, 'cause coyote win for sure."

"Well, we'll see about that, Snort. I can promise only that I'll be totally fair and square." Heh, heh. "And you go first."

They shook their heads. "Hunk go first. Coyote go fifth."

"You mean second, don't you?"

He clubbed me over the head. "Mean go fifth."

"Okay, fine. That'll work." I took a deep breath. "Well, here goes. You're going to love this one. It raises a deep philosophical point, Snort, and asks the question, 'How could a mother skunk love her children?'"

"Coyote not give hoot for deep fizzological point. Sing song, then shut up."

"Okay, fine. Here goes." And with that, I sang my new dynamite song, which, by the way, I composed on the spot. It had been more or less inspired by my encounter with Leroy the Skunk.

Ode to a Mother Skunk

I've noticed in the course of years,
A-traveling through this vale of tears,
There's several things I've never understood.
How tall's the sky, how deep's the sea?
And how come God invented me?
And how do skunks cope with motherhood?

Now, a skunk's no friend of mine, I'll say.
I'll walk around one any day.
If he takes the high road, I'll take the low.
I think that everyone agrees
That a skunk smells bad in the first degree.
So how do they fall in love, do you suppose?

Just think about it, contemplate.
Who'd ask a skunk out for a date?
A date with a skunk couldn't be much fun.
A guy would have to be pretty drunk
To spend an evening with a skunk,
And who could stand the smell to marry one?

Imagine the bride in her wedding clothes,
Wearing a clothespin on her nose,
While the groom holds his breath just to
    survive.

And if children came, heaven forbid,
Could a mother skunk really love those kids?
That couldn't make her glad to be alive.

Now, what a shock to a young girl's mind,
First to fall in love and then to find
Herself in charge of a brood of little skunks.
Now, a man would go into a coma,
Hit the roof and call his momma,
"Ma, git over here and help me pack my
    trunks!"

But a woman's love, they say, is blind
She'll give it to 'most any kind
Of ugly thing she finds in the nursery.
If a mother skunk can love those young'uns,
Smelling like a bunch of onions,
Then a mother's love can't smell, much less see.

So the next time you old moms out there
Are tired of worry, work, and care
And wondering if this motherhood really pays.
Just remember, it could be worse—
Riding to church in the back of a hearse
Or being a momma skunk on Mother's Day.

Happy Mother's Day to you,
Be glad you're not a skunk.

CHAPTER ELEVEN

The Vampire Cat Appears

~~~~~~

Well, I put my whole heart and soul into the
song, and when I'd finished, I faced Rip and
Snort and waited for a roar of applause.

They stared at me. No applause.

"Well? Is that all I get for doing the best song
of the year?"

"Not best song of year," said Snort, "only boring and stupid. Coyote not give hoot for mother
skunk."

"But you'll have to admit that the melody was
kind of nice."

They shook their heads. "Not have to admit.
Coyote song much better and betterest."

"Yeah, but you haven't even sung it yet and
it's illegal and crooked to make judgments before

95

you've done the song. Who knows, you guys might not remember your words. And don't forget who's the official judge of this contest."

I didn't like the way they laughed at that last statement. It made me wonder if they were going to keep their respective words about making this an honest contest.

Mary D must have been having the same thoughts, because she looked up at me and whispered, "I don't think this is going to work, Harvey."

"Of course it is, and will you stop calling me Harvey?"

She didn't have time to answer. Just then Rip and Snort began warming up their tonsils and preparing for their big production. And they told me to sit down and shut up, which I, uh, considered a fairly reasonable request—considering who they were and all.

So I sat down and shut my trap and listened to their latest assault on good taste and music. It had a lot of rhythm and noise and no melody whatsoever—a pretty good kind of song for cannibals, in other words, because they can't carry a tune anyway. Let's see if I can explain what they did.

They started off by laying down a basic rhythm of eight beats:

Rumble rumble rumble rumble rumble
    rumble mutter,
Rumble rumble rumble, mutter mutter.

Then Snort added the main vocals, if that's
what you call it, and it went something like this:

The Cannibal Way

Rip and Snort are toughest guys,
Singing song and telling lies.
Howl at moon and play all night,
Love to eat and love to fight.

Sleep all day, not give a hoot
Coyote just a big galoot
Better not get in our way
Or we will punch your lights out.

It's the cannibal way,
The cannibal way.
It's the cannibal, animal, fo-fan-fanibal
Cannibal way.

We see you in the dark, you know you
    can't hide.
We got eyes on the front and eyes on the side.

See, we see you, we hear you, we're coming
    on through,
The world's most famous wrecking crew.

We smell pretty bad and we know we are cool
'Cause we learned our stuff at Cannibal
    School.
Bobcats, badgers, guard-dog mutts,
We clean their clocks and kick their shins.

    It's the cannibal way,
    The cannibal way.
    It's the cannibal, animal, fo-fan-fanibal
    Cannibal way.

The brothers finished their little whatever-it-was. You can call it a song if you wish. I'd call it a noisy, tasteless piece of low-class coyote trash, every bit as bad as the others I had heard them do over the years.

They turned to me with big sloppy grins on their faces. "Now what Hunk say?"

"Well, it, uh, leaves me breathless."

"What that means, dressless?"

"It means . . . well, I guess you're wanting to hear the final opinion of our impartial panel of judges, and here it is."

I paused for a moment, just for dramatic effect, and pretended to be giving the matter deep and serious thought, although I had, uh, more or less already picked the winner.

"Okay, guys, we've got a winner. Stand by. Our big winner in tonight's contest is . . . Hank the Cowdog, doing 'Ode to a Mother Skunk'!"

No applause. Only blank stares.

"But you guys win the consolation prize, which is a one-week all-expenses-paid vacation in the next canyon. Congratulations and start moving, Kitty, these guys have been known to riot after a big defeat." We began edging northward. "And boys, it was fun, we really enjoyed it, and what really matters is not who wins or loses but . . ."

In a flash, they had changed positions and were blocking our path. Snort was grinning. "Huh! What really matter is cheat and win, then have big coyote feast."

"Yes, Snort, but that would be . . . uh, cheating. And I know that you wouldn't want history to record that you were a couple of cheaters, so to speak."

"Ha! Coyote not give hoot for so-to-speaking. Only give hoot for big yummy supper. Start with cat, then eat Hunk too, oh boy!"

Miss Kitty and I traded looks. She said, "I didn't think it would work."

"Quiet. I'm not through yet. It's going to get a little crazy from here on, so be prepared to play to my lead. And be ready to run." I turned back to Snort. "Okay, fine. Now we know the truth about you guys. You cheat and can't be trusted, and I guess that's our tough luck."

"Ha! Berry tough."

"But before you proceed with this shameless travesty of justice, there's something you should know about this cat."

"Uh. Coyote eat cat in two bites, not give hoot for shameful tapestry."

"Yeah? Well, you'd better hear me out and then you can make up your own minds. I mean, you guys are old enough now to start making your own decisions about, well, life and setting a good example for the youth of our . . ."

"Hunk get to point."

"Right, and here's the point." I left Mary D's side and walked over to the brothers, and whispered, "Boys, two nights ago, that cat was bitten on the neck by a VAMPIRE!"

There was a long moment of silence as the brothers stared at me with big empty eyes. "What means, bitten by umpire?"

"Not an umpire, Snort, a vampire. Do you know about vampires?"

He shook his head. "Coyote not play baseball, not give a hoot for fun and games."

"Yeah, well, vampires aren't fun and games." I leaned forward and spoke in my spookiest voice. "Vampires are terrible scary creatures. They rise up out of the graveyard in the deep dark of the night, and they go moaning and crying through the night, looking for victims.

"You know what they do? They bite their victim on the neck and inject them with the deadly Vampire Virus, and then they tear out the victim's throbbing gizzard . . . and EAT IT RAW!"

I studied my audience. They were all ears and eyes. They were buying the story, I could tell.

"And then, Snort, after doing all that, they turn their victim into a little squeaking mouse! Oh, and one last thing about vampires. They hate cheaters."

Snort spoke in a hoarse whisper. "Um. Coyote not crazy for meeting umpire."

"Yeah? Well, you're fixing to meet one right now. Watch this." I turned to Mary D and gave her the Secret Sign—a slightly raised eyebrow. Then I closed my eyes and said the next part in the spookiest voice I could come up with:

"Seven slithering slimy lizards,
Spiderwebs and haunted houses.

Arise, oh vampire, seek their gizzards,
And turn them into squeaking mouses!"

You might remember that Mary D had shown signs of weirdness earlier in the day. In other words, she knew a thing or two about strange behavior, and she didn't get it out of a book. She knew about it firsthand.

And once she had figgered out what I was doing, she played her part like a real pro. She rose slowly from the ground, kind of like a balloon being inflated, and as she rose her eyes grew wider and wider. And remember that she had those greenish-yellow cat eyes, the very spookiest kind when you see them in the dark.

Her eyes grew wider and wider and you know how cat eyes are sometimes black in the center? That's the way they were—two glowing circles of greenish-yellow light, with darkness at the centers.

She floated up to a standing position, and then the middle of her back kept going up, making the kind of hump that cats make when they're mad or crazy. And she opened her mouth, showed them her spiky little teeth, and cut loose with an eerie yowl.

Now, sometimes when a cat goes through all of that routine, it will cause a dog to become inflamed

and want to start barking. But Mary D was playing her part so well, and it was kind of a dark spooky night anyways and I had softened up the brothers with my vampire story—all of that together took its toll on the morale of the Cannibal Army.

Their ears shot straight up and their eyes grew as wide as saucers, and I noticed that a strip of hair was beginning to rise on both their backs. And fellers, they were watching every move she made and giving her their full attention.

In other words, they were not showing signs of inflammation, which was very good, because if they had, we would have been finished. It appeared that we had a chance of pulling it off.

Well, Mary D went on with the drama. After rising slowly to her feet and humping her back and yowling, she locked her gaze on them and took a step toward them—and hissed. It was a very convincing hiss and it caused the brothers to inch backward. And then she moaned,

"The moon is full, the earth is turning,
My vampire appetite is burning.
Two coyote gizzards I must eat
To make this dreadful night complete."

Say, that DID get their full attention, especially the part about coyote gizzards. Rip looked at Snort and Snort looked at Rip, and then he turned to me.

"Uh. Coyote not so hungry now. Maybe Hunk better call off umpire and keep away from Rip and Snort."

"Sure, good idea. I just want you guys to know . . . you're right, Snort, I'd better try to get her under control—before it's too late." I spoke to Kitty. "Get back, vampire, get back! Away, away, be gone!"

She turned and hissed at me and . . . by George,

it sent a few shivers down my backbone, even though I was part of the show.

"Hey guys, I'm afraid it's too late. Once she starts these vampire fits, she's out of control. All I can tell you is that if she comes after you with those deadly poison vampire fangs, you'd better run for your lives."

Right on cue, she sprang in their direction.

"Oh no, there she goes! She's out of control, the vampire has taken over! Run for your lives, boys, and protect your gizzards!"

There was a mad scramble, and then . . . silence. Total silence. Mary D stood alone in the moonlight. We had pulled it off.

"Nice work, Kitty."

Her head came around very slowly and . . . hmm, she stared at me with those strange eyes and . . . my goodness, then she hissed, "I AM a vampire and I want YOUR gizzard!"

CHAPTER TWELVE

I Am Turned into a Vampire! (Not Really)

HUH?

The old ears shot straight up and the old eyes popped open. I felt the hair rise on the back of my neck as I, uh, went to Full Reverse on all engines and more or less dug four trenches in the snow.

Then she smiled. "Just kidding. I'll have to remember this vampire routine. It works like a charm."

I managed to get everything shut down before I tore down any trees or caused any major damage to the surrounding ecosystems. I studied her very carefully.

"Are you kidding or not?"

"Of course I'm kidding. How could I turn into a vampire?"

"Well, a guy never knows about you cats, and don't forget whose idea it was, and stop using my ideas against me. It's not funny."

"Sorry. I just couldn't resist."

"Okay. Let's get out of here before they decide to come back. Lead the way."

She went scampering up the canyon—across a snowy meadow, over rocks and through bushes, and then into a forest of huge cedar trees. I soon lost my sense of direction, and I could only hope that this crazy cat knew where she was going.

At last we came to the place she had called Moonshine Springs, where clear sweet water came out from under a big rock. We paused there to catch our breath and get a drink. Then she pointed to a washed-out trail going up the side of the canyon wall.

"That's the only way out."

"Boy, that's a steep rascal. I hope . . ."

Suddenly I was cut off in mid-sentence by the raspy hacksaw voice of . . . yikes, was it Rip and Snort?

"Hey, y'all can't leave! We ain't had a bite to eat in three whole days, we're starved plumb out, and . . . Junior, talk to 'em, son, and explain just how hungry we are."

I seemed to remember hearing that voice before. It belonged to a certain buzzard named Wallace, who happened to have a son named Junior. Yes, it was all fitting together.

I swept the surrounding trees with my most penetrating radar gaze and . . . sure enough, there they were, perched on the limb of a big cottonwood tree—two slouching, hungry buzzards.

Junior grinned and waved his wing at me. "Oh, h-hi D-d-doggie. W-w-w-we g-got lost in the n-n-night."

"Yes we did," said Wallace, "got lost and blowed off course in the snowstorm, and here we are in

108

this canyon. Tell 'em how hungry we are, son."

"W-we're l-lost and p-p-pretty h-hungry."

"Very hungry, Junior. We were *pretty* hungry two days ago and ain't had a scrap to eat since then." Wallace glared down at me. "We're *very* hungry, is what Junior's tryin' to say, and I don't suppose y'all would happen to have, oh, a couple of pounds of baloney or some old chicken necks you don't need, or a dead rabbit, would you?"

"Nope. We're on our way back to the home ranch and we've got no eats. Sorry."

"Naw you ain't. You don't give a care. You're just sayin' that."

"Okay. We don't have any eats and I don't give a care."

"See there, Junior! I knew he didn't care and that's the kind of friends you have, selfish and heartless, and . . ." His eyes focused on Mary D Cat, who had begun rubbing on my leg. "Say, neighbor, what do we have there?"

"This," I said, moving away from the rubbing machine, "is a cat, and she will rub on anything."

A sparkle came into his eyes. "A cat, a darling little kitty cat! You know, if that cat's gettin' on your nerves, maybe we could talk trade."

"Oh n-now P-pa, d-d-don't s-start that. The k-k-kitty is his f-f-f-friend, m-most likely."

"Hush, son, I'm a-workin' on a deal here." Wallace turned back to me. "Anyways, dog, me and Junior was just a-wonderin' about the maybe-so of makin' a little swap for that cat of yours."

Junior rolled his eyes. "Oh P-p-pa, d-d-don't embarrass m-m-me again!"

The old man ignored him. "That's a mighty nice looking cat, neighbor, and me and Junior would sure try to trade with you."

I chuckled. "Oh, you wouldn't like this cat, Wallace. Every once in a while she turns into a vampire."

There was a moment of silence. "A vampire! You mean, one of them thangs that bites necks and drinks blood?"

"Right, and this one just loves gizzards."

There was another moment of silence. "Gizzards! Now, just hold your horses, pooch, that's kind of backwards to what we had in mind."

I gave Mary D the raised eyebrow She shifted into her Floating and Moaning Routine and cast a hungry look up into the tree.

"The moon is full, the earth is turning,
My vampire appetite is burning.
Two buzzard gizzards I must eat
To make this dreadful night complete."

Wallace bought the whole show—hook, line, and sawhorse. "Son, I think that pretty much answers all the questions I had about vampires, and I reckon we'd better... spread your wings, son, we're fixing to catch a plane out of here."

"I thought w-we were g-g-going to s-s-s-spend the n-night here, P-p-pa."

"Son, a guy can always find another cotton-wood tree, but his gizzard is very close to his heart, and no, we ain't staying the night here with all these vampires runnin' around, let's go."

"But Wallace," I said, trying to hide a smile, "I thought you wanted to work a trade."

"No sir, I did not, that was all Junior's idea. I ain't hungry, couldn't hold another bite, and while a buzzard will eat 'most anything that moves, we draw the line at vampires, and son, I'm a-quitting this place, see you upstairs."

With that, he spread his wings, pushed off of the limb, and went flapping into the night sky. Junior grinned and shook his head.

"I th-think y-you g-g-g-got 'im on that one, D-d-d-doggie."

"Yeah, well, I owed him one. See you around, Junior. I'm sorry we didn't have a chance to sing."

"M-m-maybe n-next t-time, next time. B-b-bye, D-doggie."

He crouched down on the limb, gave a jump, flapped his big buzzard wings as hard as he could, took the top out of a cedar tree, and vanished into the darkness.

I chuckled to myself and noticed that Mary D was watching me with a little smile on her mouth. "You've really enjoyed this vampire business, haven't you?"

"A guy has to make his fun where he can, Kitty. And yes, life's liable to seem pretty dull if I ever get around normal dogs and cats and people again."

"Oh, so you're going to blame it all on me?"

I whopped her on the back. "Why not? That's what cats are for. Now, let's see if we can find our way back to the ranch."

We made our way out of the deep spooky darkness of Picket Canyon, which was no small deal, let me tell you. We had to climb almost straight up over rocks and snow, mountains, glaciers, and so forth, but at last we made it over the rim.

Once on the flats, we stopped to catch our breaths. A gentle breeze was blowing out of the southwest, an indication that the storm had passed. The clouds had rolled away, leaving a black velvet sky speckled with diamonds of light.

"Holy smokes, just look at those stars! If a guy

spent enough time looking at those things, it would almost make him feel humble about his place in the world."

"Almost?"

"Yeah, well, in my line of work, a guy can't use too much of that stuff. There's not much demand for humble dogs in the . . . you seem to be rubbing on me again. Have we discussed my feelings about being rubbed on by cats?"

She was rubbing on my front legs and flipping that tail across my nose. "I know what you think, Harvey, but I wanted to rub you good-bye."

"Good-bye? What do you mean, good-bye? I thought . . ."

"Oh, I know. I made such a scene about being marooned and wanting to leave, but now that I'm free to leave . . . my goodness, it seems that the free-dom to leave was more important than the leaving."

"The freedom was more . . . hmm."

"Yes, and now that I'm free to leave, I'm also free to stay, and I think I will. After all, who'd want to go back to civilization and become a normal cat?" She smiled a crazy smile and stared at me with those big cattish eyes. "Being weird is really fun."

"Well, you ought to be having a ball, sister, because you win the prize for weirdness. And you made a very convincing vampire."

"Wasn't that fun! I may try it out on Leroy. Oh, won't he be surprised?"

She chuckled and dived back into rubbing on my legs. I stared at her and shook my head.

"You know, I never thought I'd be teamed up with a cat. It kind of wrecks my whole theory of life. I mean, if there's one good cat in the world, everything's up for grabs."

She turned her face up to me and batted her eyelids. "Maybe everything IS up for grabs. Or maybe I'm not such a good cat. Tomorrow, I might want to tear out your eyeballs."

"Yeah, and that could get you turned into kitty hamburger. But tonight, right now, this minute, you're okay, Kitty. Just don't ever tell anybody I said so. It could ruin my reputation."

She rubbed me one last time. "Good-bye, Harvey."

"Good-bye, Gertrude."

"My name's Mary D."

"My name's Hank."

"You're nice—for a dog."

"You're nice—for a vampire."

And with that, I set my course by the North Star, waved a last good-bye, and began the long trip back.

Case closed.

And don't you DARE tell anybody that I made friends with a cat!

Have you read all of Hank's adventures?

Join Hank the Cowdog's Security Force

Are you a big Hank the Cowdog fan? Then you'll want to join Hank's Security Force. Here is some of the neat stuff you will receive:

Welcome Package
- A Hank paperback of your choice
- Free Hank bookmarks

Eight issues of *The Hank Times* with
- Stories about Hank and his friends
- Lots of great games and puzzles
- Special previews of future books
- Fun contests

More Security Force Benefits
- Special discounts on Hank books and audiotapes
- An original Hank poster (19" x 25") absolutely free
- Unlimited access to Hank's Security Force website at www.hankthecowdog.com

Total value of the Welcome Package and *The Hank Times* is $23.95. However, your two-year membership is **only $8.95** plus $3.00 for shipping and handling.

☐ Yes, I want to join Hank's
Security Force. Enclosed
is $11.95 ($8.95 + $3.00
for shipping and handling)
for my **two-year member-
ship**. [Make check payable
to Maverick Books.]

**Which book would you like to receive in your
Welcome Package? Choose from any book in
the series.**

(#   )   (#   )
_____
FIRST CHOICE   SECOND CHOICE

                                            BOY or GIRL
_____
YOUR NAME   (CIRCLE ONE)

_____
MAILING ADDRESS

_____
CITY   STATE   ZIP

_____
TELEPHONE   BIRTH DATE

_____
E-MAIL

Are you a ☐ Teacher or ☐ Librarian?

Send check or money order for $11.95 to:

Hank's Security Force
Maverick Books
P.O. Box 549
Perryton, Texas 79070

DO NOT SEND CASH. NO CREDIT CARDS ACCEPTED.
Allow 4–6 weeks for delivery.

The Hank the Cowdog Security Force, the Welcome Package, and The
Hank Times _are the sole responsibility of Maverick Books. They are not
organized, sponsored, or endorsed by Penguin Putnam Inc., Puffin Books,
Viking Children's Books, or their subsidiaries or affiliates._